Troubles
In My Way

VOLUME I

I AM A TRUE BELIEVER THAT LIFE IS NOT ABOUT WAITING FOR THE STORM TO PASS, BUT LEARNING HOW TO MAKE A JOYFUL NOISE EVEN THOUGH THE SKY'S ARE GRAY!

Troubles
In My Way

VOLUME I

Witness a complete transformation from Trials, Tribulations and Troubles....to Triumph

---

VIVIAN D. LEWIS

authorHOUSE®

AuthorHouse™
1663 Liberty Drive
Bloomington, IN 47403
www.authorhouse.com
Phone: 1-800-839-8640

All Scripture quotations are taken from the King James Version of the Bible.

Published by AuthorHouse   09/07/2012

ISBN: 978-1-4772-6329-7 (sc)
ISBN: 978-1-4772-6328-0 (e)

Library of Congress Control Number: 2012915693

Any people depicted in stock imagery provided by Thinkstock are models, and such images are being used for illustrative purposes only.
Certain stock imagery © Thinkstock.

This book is printed on acid-free paper.

FOR INFORMATION CONTACT:
Vivian Lewis
(210) 384-2719
vivianlewis32@yahoo.com
http://www.facebook.com/vivianfoxiebrownlewis

VIVIAN "LADY V" LEWIS
"Troubles in My Way" is reverenced to our most powerful savior for allowing me the opportunity to share how life can take us through twist and turns . . . .

*But when we seek
God for
righteousness, he will
began to straighten
out our path for
divined destination.*

*TO GOD ALL THE
GLORY IS GIVEN"*

Acknowledgements

I reverence all praises to God for the ability and opportunity to share this reality of life.

"Troubles in my Way" is comprised of Trials, Tribulations, Troubles and Triumph. We as humans will always have struggles and heavy burdens but as we follow the great book of the kingdom we conform to a different understanding and style of life.

I want to Thank my loving family, Hattie Clay (mother) for encouraging me to always be obedient and listen when God speak, Kevin Jerome Lewis (deceased) for being my angel of comfort, Brandon Michael Lewis (son) for being my everything, Willie Mae White and Patricia Lewis (sisters) standing on the promises of God,

Brian Lewis (nephew) and my loving grandsons, Keevontae Jerome Lewis and baby (Houston Lewis deceased).

Special Thanks to the late Dr. E.Thurman Walker and Lady Jo Angelia Walker for extending their love to our family and teaching me the proper way to adhere to the great fight of life. Dr. Kenneth Kemp and first Lady Velma Kemp Thank you for the continued leadership towards my spiritual growth, I am so blessed to be under the authority of such a divined Shepherd, the power within me is anchored.

Special Recognition: Rodney "Sir Bizzle" Warner Jr. Global Acclaimed Recording Artist for being a great listener and for encouraging me to take my skills, talents and dreams to the top.

Clinton and Joyce Warner Wiggins, DeGerald and Crystal Price, Jacob and Sharita Baker and Cinnamon Warner, Thank you for being my inspirational connection and showing so much love and concern.

Bernard and Angelia Jollivette, Thank you for extending your family to my family when we joined Antioch Baptist Church, 20 years ago. Sister Jollivette Thank you for singing "Jesus will Work it out", it kept me pressing forward.

Delores "Mama Dee" Williams, Thank you for allowing me to grow in the music ministry, the songs that I lead "Lord, Lord, Lord You been Blessing Me" and "It's your Season" are my two inspirations when times get tough, I appreciate you believing in me and allowing God to work through me, It changed me!

Lastly, to my SPECIAL friends, Zelphia Davis Beverly, Deborah Nobles, Arneca Green, Leroy Morrow, Dr. Lilian Haffner, Rachel Pickett, Sherryl Murray, Donald Jones, Princess County, Robert & Anita Williams, Larry Williams, Charles & Sandra Johnson and Pamela Kennon, Thank you for sticking by my side and always giving me encouragement to strive for excellence.

Love,
Vivian Lady "V" Lewis

Jesus Thank you for all that you have done for me . . . allowing me to see the forest through the trees . . . . NOW I BELIEVE!

Psalm 1:2, 3 Because I delight in
God's law I am like a tree that yields
in season and whose leaf does not
wither. Whatever I do prospers!

WOMAN WITH THE POWER WITHIN

LADY "V"

TABLE OF CONTENTS

LORD LEAD ME
GUIDE ME EVERYDAY
AND DON'T LET ME
STRAY

GOD IS OUR REFUGE & STRENGTH, A VERY PRESENT HELP IN TIMES OF TROUBLE - PSALM 46:1

INTRODUCTION

DO YOU OR SOMEONE YOU KNOW HAVE TROUBLES IN THEIR WAY . . . . EVERYDAY STRUGGLES . . . . UNWISE CHOICES . . . . NO PEACE . . . . NO HAPPINESS . . . . NEAR DEATH . . . .

We often dream of having a perfect family—father, mother, two children and a big house with a White Pickett fence . . . . as we transform into reality, we strive to live the life of our dream . . . . well . . . . all that sounds GREAT . . . . BUT it only take ONE "THING" to tear down the walls of our dream and SHATTER IT INTO PEICES . . . .

Witness a GRUESOME HIT ROCK BOTTOM TRAGEDY within a SO CALLED perfect family, watch as they go through "TREMENDOUS" TRIALS, TRIBULATIONS, AND EYE OPENING TROUBLES then WITNESS THE ONE "THING" THAT WILL make a complete transformation into TRIUMPH . . . .

Chapter One

"TRIALS"

Anger, anger, anger my way of life, my
emotional journey began as a child, domestic
violence within my family, financial
struggles and no parenting structure . . . .

My mother tried very hard to maintain a
balanced home but problems always tore us
apart. My father was an alcoholic, cheater
and con man that made people around him
miserable including his family, everyday
anger and name calling. My sister LaLa and
I hated living in the house because we knew
something would always happen. No Peace!
No Comfort!

My mother worked day labor to make sure
we had a roof over our head and food on
our table; my father did not contribute to the
household without anger, aggression and
abuse, he was a thief and a manipulator.

When I turned twelve my mother made the statement, "I'm tired and I can't take no more, Now that you are old enough to understand, I'm divorcing your father". She continued by saying "I took years of battering, bruises, black eyes, tormenting and vulgar language, just to keep my family together, it was not pleasant. Your daddy was in and out of the household taking what little we had, somewhere else". Once again anger erupted in our household.

After the divorce, mama filed child support to help with the financial struggle. Daddy did not accept the fact that he had to pay for us to live, he called my mother and told her if she didn't stop filing and harassing him for money he would blow our house up, while we sleep. Mama being the smart women that she was did not take any chances and dropped the child support case. Once again anger and frustration erupted in our household, mama became bitter started smoking and drinking, staying out late. No Peace! No Comfort!

My sister and I stayed at home with constant fear because mama was not home. It became very obvious that mama started changing her life out of anger from the divorce, she felt like her life was over and she had no reason to live. The trials, tribulations and troubles that she was experiencing were destroying our home and our relationship, with her. Every day drunk and high from Marijuana, she lost her strength and faith; she did not speak of God anymore.

Early one Saturday morning, mama finally came home, I met her at the door and she appeared to have been beat up. Her clothes were muddy, dirty and torn, she also had black eyes. I asked her what happened, she replied "nothing" and go to bed. I went to my room crying because right before my eyes my mama turned from a godly loving woman and parent to a faithless drug user, drinking until she passed out.

I didn't quite understand how she could change like that. I never thought I would see my loving mother turn into a beast.

I was too young to understand how mama was tormented for all those years while married to daddy and she kept living like that. Our home was destroyed, our family was destroyed and we all had emotional problems.

Mama went so low she stopped working everyday, not caring how the bills got paid. I got a job to help make ends meet, thinking that would make our household better but more problems occurred. My sister LaLa now age fourteen, started experiencing abnormal behavior, getting in trouble at school, went from being an honor student to failing. Now I not only have mama with extreme dysfunction, but now my baby sister had problems.

I seem to be the only mentally stable person in our house. I turned from a young teenager to an adult with responsibilities. I tried to continue in school, go to work and now, the head of the household; mama could not make any decisions.

I didn't understand why our home was so messed up, I often felt everybody was so happy, but my family. I remembered when we were young, mama took us to church, our pastor spoke on trials, tribulations and troubles, and he reassured us that after the storm was all over, triumph was a new beginning. He went on to say "seek God first and everything else would be added unto you! He will open up the windows of heaven and pour out many blessings; we will not have room enough to receive it! Keep the faith, remain strong, think positive and don't give up"!

I kept hearing those words over and over in my head. It gave me the encouragement and strength to step up as an adult, go to school, take care of mama, the house and be a parent to my sister. I said to the lord "I'm only sixteen, can I do this"? The voice in my head replied "you are the way, I told you I would never put too much on you, that you could not handle. Step up and take care of business, your blessings will come".

In spite of all the problems that continued
to occur daily, I knew the words in my
head were God giving me strength to keep
pushing forward. I knew my life and my
family would get better, God told me to
never lose faith.

Mama continued to cry, blaming herself
for the horrible divorce. She felt if she had
stayed with daddy, her life would not have
been the way it was. I didn't understand
completely why she felt being mentally and
physically abused, was the proper way of
life; she divorced him because it was not
the way of life. I asked mama why she was
blaming herself, for all the destruction of our
family when she was the one that kept it all
together.

I also told her that daddy destroyed our
home and our lives, the enemy is against us,
but God is for us. We must put the miserable
past behind us and move on to a bright and
meaningful future, but first we must bring
back the power of God into our home.

We must allow God to take control again just as he did when we were younger, we all fall down sometimes, but we don't have to stay down. I ask you mama to "please give up the drugs and the drinking, go to rehab and start a new beginning, it's not too late".
Mama and I were crying knowing the struggles were so tremendously devastating and I knew we could not handle it all alone. I wondered if mama had completely lost her faith, she was so down on herself.

I received a call because LaLa skipped school and ended up in jail under a ten-thousand dollar bond for participating in the robbery of our neighborhood convenience store. Well here I go again, being a stand in parent, mama was no where to be found, I went to the jail all alone. When, I saw my sister she had black eyes, bruises, and scrapes to her skin. I was crying, angry and devastated because my daddy caused our family to be torn apart.

Mama used to be a woman of God and LaLa was an honor roll student, she instilled in me at an early age how important it was to stay focused on Jesus, so my strength would remain strong. I tried to keep the words in my head but the pain grew stronger and stronger. I kept telling myself everyday, don't give up, and keep my head up.

LaLa was released after I paid six-hundred dollars. She was very quiet, hanging her head low. I asked her why she felt she needed to rob when she knew that was against the word of God and one of the Ten Commandments, "Thou shall not steal". Her reply was "I don't know! He made me!"

I said "who made you, what are you talking about"? LaLa dropped her head even lower and became non-talkative. I started shouting, "talk to me, and tell me LaLa who made you rob the store? What is wrong and why do you have black eyes and bruises?" She said "this man that I confided in took advantage of me, raped me and gave me money and made me do drugs".

I asked her how long had she been involved with this person, her reply was "nine months, he treated me so nice in the beginning then started making me do wrong things" he also said he would kill me if I didn't do what he said".

My sister was only fifteen years old . . . .

Lala and I got home, settled in, when all of a sudden the phone rang, it was the police department calling to say, mama was locked up in the county jail under a thirty thousand dollar bond for soliciting her body for money to purchase drugs.

HERE I GO AGAIN . . . .

I asked God "what do I do, it is too much I'm only eighteen and I can't take it no more". The little voice in my head said "you can handle this; I have given you the power to handle any and everything, go to your mother help her". Six hours passed, mama was released after I paid sixteen hundred dollars.

I told mama with a loud shout, that her life must change! She made no reply as her head hung low, crying ecstatically. Mama started screaming "I'm tired, I'm tired, I'm tired, help me lord, take me and renew my strength".

Six months passed mama agreed to go talk to a counselor. She enrolled in a program called Positive Directions; a new life beginning which taught her how to overcome trials, tribulations, and troubles, the end result would be triumph (victory) a new rejuvenation of life . . . . I was so happy because I new I would have my mama back. She attended four months group therapy started progressing, minimal drinking and no drugs and had a positive outlook on life when all of a sudden she relapsed, but this time she took by baby sister LaLa, with her.

I could not believe my eyes as I walked to the store, I saw both of them on the outside of a building, sitting on a couch passing a pipe from one to the other. Through devastation and fear I immediately ran and knocked the pipe from my mothers hand as she was passing it to LaLa.

She got very angry with a look to kill on her
face. LaLa was crying and screaming loudly
telling me I should mind my own business.
I told her, she was my business and before
I see my sixteen year old sister die in the
streets I would put her in lockup. I did not
know what to do, I was out numbered, my
mother and sister, doing drugs together.

I looked up in the sky and said "God help
me now, I need to hear from you, I'm tired
and I'm worn, I have no life just troubles. All
my struggles seem to be because of others,
I can't take it anymore lord". The voice in
my head said "yes you can, take control and
always remember I am God, I rule the world
I'm here with you. I never told you it would
be easy and I never told you that you would
get everything you asked for right away, but
I did tell you to keep the faith, carry on my
child".

I pulled mama and LaLa up from the couch
when I was approached by a man telling me
I wasn't taking them nowhere without being
paid eight hundred dollars for drug charges.
I told him I would pay him and to never give
them anymore drugs.

Immediately, the man said "lady this is my business, pay up and get them broke sleaze bags out of here. If you ever come back and try to stop my flow, you will regret it". I did not know if I was going to make it out alive, but I knew God had my back, I refused to leave my mama and sister there to die.

By the time we made it home both mama and LaLa had passed out. Morning came, I had to go to school and work, mama and LaLa remained sleep. LaLa missed another day of school and failing all her subjects, I decided to tell the school she was sick again, I sure hated to lie.

I decided to confide in my pastor about what was happening at home. Pastor Getitrite told me he was very concerned about our family because he hadn't seen any of us at church in months. I told him I needed some advice and guidance on how to get our family back together. After several meetings pastor told me I have to do for me and send plenty of prayer for my family, but to never give up on them.

I must continue to do what I can to help them but make sure I am getting the spiritual food I need to help myself; I decided to take his advice.

Six months passed mama hit rock bottom had to be hospitalized for an overdose of Cocaine. The doctor told her she was very lucky to be alive after all the drugs found in her system. Mama had numerous needle marks on her arms. Days passed, mama was recovering; she continued to tell me how thankful she was to have me as her daughter.

LaLa returned to school four days ago, but never made it. I received a call from them asking me were she still sick and all I could say, again was yes. I went to the place where I saw her last, but she was not there. I called the police missing persons unit, but they seem to have been unconcerned. The deputy said "those darn kids do what they want to and don't listen to their parents".

I decided to take the advice of my pastor and focus on me, I went to the club met a man named John and after conversation, drinks and dinner I gave him my phone number. It sure felt good to finally get away from everybody else's problems and focus on myself. John and I developed a friendship, we went to the midnight movies, and ate out late at night. I asked him if he was married, his reply was *no,* I asked him if he had a girlfriend, he said *no*.

I began interacting with him more enjoying his companionship and late night conversations. After two months of continuous talking, it felt so good to finally have a good friend, someone that was interested in me, not just for sex and he helped relieve the stress from the problems associated with mama and LaLa.

Two weeks passed LaLa still missing, no contact. Where could she be? I went to the missing person's office in hopes she may have been found. I was informed that no one by the name of LaLa Sorento was noted as missing.

Mama got out of the hospital today and made the statement "I'm so tired, I don't have anything to live for. My life was completely destroyed. Why, why, why me lord, why am I going through all this pain, I was a good person, I was in church but I totally fell so low, I'm a wreck, I want to die!" I could not stand to hear her talking like that anymore.

I told mama to stop saying those bad things, God will never leave us, but he will allow us to make choices. "Mama please go back to group counseling, look at what your life did to LaLa, now she's a drug user, a prostitute and she's missing. Our family is dysfunctional; if you change our family will get better. I beg you to stop and get help".

After three weeks disappearance, LaLa appeared at midnight with black eyes, bruises, scratches and dirty clothes. She looked like an old woman. She was begging for food and money. Mama began crying loudly after she saw her baby child's face destroyed, arms scraped up and her hair matted to her head.

I look at her and nodded my head saying "my sister just sixteen years old, with a messed up life". I was glad both of them were at home, I felt this could be the beginning of rekindling our family.

After four weeks of no conversation with John, the phone rang; it was him calling late at night. I was so happy to hear his voice. He stated he was out of town with his job and would return in two days. I was so glad to hear from him, I did not question his whereabouts anymore.

One thing that did cross my mind was, even though he was out of town he could have called, the conversation continued, he told me he was sorry for not calling, but he had been real busy. I told him that I understood and I did forgive him. I had began to develop an interest in him, I also told him I missed him and I wanted to see him, he said I would see him as soon as he get back because he missed me too. Wow, what a good feeling!

Two days passed and I did not hear from
John, I did not have a phone number where
I could call him, he told me he did not have
a home phone and he couldn't remember his
work number. He said he would give it to
me the next time, we saw each other. That
was three months ago. Now two more weeks
have passed, I still haven't heard from him. I
couldn't understand what was going on.

I believed in him, my first love. Unclear
thoughts began to run through my mind if
he was really a nice guy or was he lying to
me. Another week passed and at midnight
the phone ranged, it was John. He again
apologized for not calling; he said his job
kept him out of town longer. We met for a
late night meal, I was so happy to see him!
After we finished our meal I told him I was
not ready to go home, I wanted to spend
more time with him so I could get to know
him better. His reply was "I only have thirty
minutes left and I have to be back at work".

Well, it finally happened, my life has changed forever. I was in the back seat of my car but I didn't care, I felt so loved. Within ten minutes, I took him back to his car which was parked outside a convenience store; he said he had to go back to work. Now I'm in love!

Mama decided to admit herself in a rehab, she said she would not leave because she wanted to get her life back, she saw how problems caused our family to fall by the way side, she also saw how it destroyed her faith in Jesus Christ and how it destroyed her baby daughters life. I began to praise God; I said "one down, one to go, Thank you Jesus"!

LaLa slept for days as she was recovering from the wounds on her face and body. I was glad she was home; I told her that mama was in rehab and she needed to go too. She began crying telling me how sorry she was for creating all her problems, she also said she was tired of being beat up.

I told her that she had her whole life ahead
of her and if she goes to the rehab, she and
mama could encourage each other. At first,
LaLa hesitated with a not so sure look on her
face, then she said "ok lets do this" I began
screaming and crying as I was putting her
junk in the car. I knew God was beginning
to answer my prayers like he said he would.
I arrived at the rehab, checked her in and
was surprised to know she was accepted so
quickly, no paperwork needed. I didn't think
anything of it; I just wanted help for my
sister.

I couldn't believe I finally had the house to
myself quiet, peaceful and lonely. All of a
sudden the phone rang, it was John saying
he missed me and wanted to see me again.
I wondered why he always called late at
night. I told him he could come over because
I missed him too and I needed him. When
he arrived at the door, I ran up hugged him,
kissed him and blurted out, "I love you".
He had a strange look on his face but I
overlooked that because I wanted to have a
good night.

I thought about asking him to move in
since mama and LaLa was gone for a while
but I didn't know him that well. We were
passionately connected again and again,
when he left he told me he would call me the
next day, but he didn't. I got real sad because
he never kept his word.

One week passed and I did not hear from
John, two hours later the phone rang, it was
him, he said he was out of town again. I felt
so good after I heard his voice. This time, I
did not ask him why he did not contact me,
because, I was so in love. He could tell me
the sky was green and I would have believed
him, as far as I was concerned he could do
no wrong.

How blindsided could I have been . . . .

Four weeks passed, I received a knock at
my door. A lady asked me if I knew John
Adams, my reply was "why what's wrong,
is he sick, did my boyfriend get into a car
wreck? What's wrong with John and where
is he"? The lady said "My name is Jordan
Adams and I saw your name and number in
my husband's pocket.

Chapter Two

"TRIBULATIONS"

I also saw explicit letters from you. I felt
he was being unfaithful and I knew I would
finally catch him. We have five children and
I want you to know, you are one of the many
women that he is seeing. I felt like he had
been cheating on me for a long time, but I
couldn't prove it". I said "you are who, his
wife; John said he was single and had no
children" and how did you get my letters"?

Her reply was "I told you out of his pocket,
he came home drunk and I searched his
clothing". I said to myself, now what have I
got myself into, I couldn't believe the man I
fell in love with, lied to me. My heart began
beating very rapidly; the tears of betrayal
began to flow. How heart broken I was, my
first love was a dog!

Two weeks passed, John called stating he
was still out of town and how happy he was
to hear my voice. He did not know, I knew
he was married. I continued talking; waiting
for him to tell me the truth, so I told him I
couldn't wait to see him.

He arrived within the next thirty minutes,
late at night as usual, telling me how much
he missed me, he had feelings for me and
he was glad he had met me. I continued to
listen to all his lies with tears in my eyes
about how much he enjoyed me and how
I was going to be his future wife and baby
mama. It felt very strange to listen to him but
I didn't want him to know I was on to him. I
looked at him and all I saw was a liar.

John began fondling me; I got weak and
gave in, I had developed feelings for him in
more ways than one. He told me he had to go
back to work, my heart over took my head
knowing he was married and a liar too. After
he left, I began thinking about how crazy and
stupid I was, he lied to me, could have gotten
me killed and I still gave in to him. I was
very foolish and weak to know he was using
me and I continued to allow him to fulfill
his pleasure. I said to myself, life is so hard,
I was lonely and I needed to be touched so
why am I feeling so bad. I got just what I
needed and from who I wanted it from, I
should be happy.

After a short pause I began thinking again about him being married, even though he said he was single. I had been completely blindsided, but it felt good. I asked the Lord "why can't I resist temptation"? His reply was "you are not listening to me; you are doing it your way. I still love you but until you pay attention to what I have asked you to do, you will always falter". I knew he was telling me the truth but I didn't want to here that.

I decided to relax for a while, when all of a sudden the phone ranged, it was John's wife asking me if her husband was with me and to let her speak to him. I told her he was not with me and that I had not heard from him, I lied. She said "woman I know you are lying because, I saw his phone records where he called you hours ago". My reply was "Jordan, Mrs. Adam's who ever yo name is; you better go look somewhere else for your man because he ain't here. If you was a good wife and taking care of his needs he wouldn't be running around on you, so go look or call somebody else". I also told her "don't you ever call here again", I hung up the phone.

I couldn't understand how she said my
number was on his phone when he said he
didn't have one, another lie. Ten minutes
later the phone rang again, his wife stating
"you better watch your back, because I will
get you". I will not allow my family to be
destroyed, I will kill for my husband", the
phone hung up.

I decided the first thing I would do when
morning came, was buy me a gun because If
and when she roll up on me, I would splatter
her all over the ground. I'm not a punk; I
will take control of the matter. After the call
the doorbell rang; I said to myself who could
that be this early in the morning, it was John.
I asked him where was he going and why
didn't he call first, his reply was "I don't
know, but I'm here now.

I thought about telling him about the phone
call, from his wife but I decided to keep
quiet because I didn't want to cause an
argument. He got in my bed and here we go,
again and again. We woke up and the sun
was shining bright, John jumped up and said
"I'm late for work"! I said to him "I thought
you worked at night?

John replied by saying "I do but I was suppose to go in early, I have to go"! He was running as he was putting his clothes on. When he left I said to my self, he's a*   *   *liar, I will get him for lying to me. I said those words out of anger but my heart felt different. I really had to think about what I was saying; I knew if I caused trouble with him, then all my pleasures, would be gone.

I also thought that if I had a part of him that would be enough. John made me feel like a woman should, I needed him. I knew at this point I was confused because I continue to give in to a man that is married and is a liar. I kept asking myself, is that all I'm worth, a moments of pleasure? I began to feel sad because he was the first man I had ever been with.

It's been four weeks since mama and LaLa had been in rehab. I was so surprised when I saw them, they looked so different, mama gained some weight and LaLa had recovered from her facial inflictions.

Wow, what a big difference!

I asked mama and LaLa, how they were doing and that I was so happy to see them on the right path. I was very happy to know our family was finally moving in a positive direction. I spent hours with them, loving every minute if it, this was a family reunion.

Just as I arrived back home, the phone was ringing, it was John. My heart began to beat fast; knowing that the man, whom I fell in love with, took my virginity and laid me down on a park table, was a liar. I couldn't resist anymore so before he could say a word I told him I knew he was married, he began stuttering.

I was determined to not let him speak so I told him he was a liar and I talked to his wife. Out of anger, I also told him to never call me again. He kept saying how sorry he was and he wanted to make it up to me, he wanted to come over, part of me wanted to say yes, but I said "No John, how could you call me after you totally destroyed me and you have lied over and over. Oh by the way I thought you didn't have a phone".

I felt so ashamed to have followed my
pastor's advice but in the wrong way. He
told me to start doing something different;
I did not think biblically, I thought worldly,
that is a big difference. Now, I have caused
all types of trials, tribulations and troubles
for myself. I am so confused; I thought that
was the right thing to do, it felt so right.
Now I'm depressed, embarrassed, have low
self esteem, sad and feel betrayed because I
couldn't believe I stooped so low.

All alone, I sat in my room, mama and LaLa
in rehab, the house was quiet, I was lonely
so I decided to take a drink from our bar. I
couldn't show my face in public after being
so stupid. I felt that everybody was looking
at me. I took a drink of Hennessy to ease
the pain. My mind kept telling me to take
another and another, before I knew it, I drank
the whole bottle.

I started feeling better; I didn't care, because
I was hurt. My head was spinning and
spinning; I needed more so I decided to go to
the club.

Upon arrival, I saw people that I knew. I went to the bar and immediately started drinking one after the other. After one hour I passed out and woke up in a strange room. I looked around the room, jumped up ran to the door and could not open it. I historically started crying yelling "where am I, where am I, I couldn't even understand how I got here.

More trials, tribulations and troubles . . . .

I heard the sounds jingling at the door, a man walked in holding a gun. I flopped down in the corner of the room crying, holding my head down. The man said, "Hold your head up sucker"! I looked up in fear and asked him "why am I here"? He replied "you stole my money", I said "I stole your money" he said "yes my money and you gon pay for it"

He also said "you were drinking at the bar and I laid my wallet down and you stole it, give it back or I'll kill you and leave you here to die, give it back"!

I continued to try and make him understand that I did not take his wallet. I told him "maybe you dropped it, maybe you left it in your car or maybe you left it at the bar" I also said "I'm not a thief, I'm a god fearing woman and one of the ten commandments is thou shall not steal". I feared for my life, but then again in the back of my mind God had my back, I just needed to remain cool.

I began to look all around and I couldn't find my purse either. I asked him "where is my purse, what did you do with my purse, how did I get here and where is my car"? His reply was "you're asking too many questions slut and you're a nasty drunk thief. I took advantage of you last night because you stole my wallet, I will teach you a lesson." I asked him "what did you do to me", he said "I raped you and I have HIV, when you steal you pay for your actions.

I began crying and pleading with the man to let me go, I also said "you raped me and you have HIV. I don't have your wallet, I'm not a thief and now you want me to live the rest of my life with the disease, all because you think I stole your wallet".

I kept talking and he said "shut up before I put the barrel of this gun down your throat, women I hate them, I have been treated badly too many times to let you go". I wanted to say more to him, but I told my self to stay quiet. After ten minutes of silence, I said "sir maybe you left your wallet at the bar". He said "I laid my wallet on the bar, went to the piss house and when I returned it was gone, the only one that saw my wallet was you".

I pleaded with him to call the bar, he said "lady if I call the bar and they don't have my wallet, you're dead". I kept quiet, praying in my mind, I said god please hear me right now, I need a miracle. Please spare my life, let this man find his wallet. Suddenly, he said "you're in luck, my wallet was found in the men's piss room".

He immediately left, leaving the door wide open, I looked all around but couldn't find my clothes; I had a t-shirt on, so I decided to make a skirt from the sheet that was on the bed. I was thanking God for hearing my plea and sparing my life, I left that horrible place.

I stopped at a nearby bus stop, sat down
to catch my breath when all of a sudden a
woman approached me stating she saw me
running and thought I may have been in
trouble. She asked me if I was o.k. I told her
I was scared, she appeared to be a nice and
kind woman, she also asked me why was I
wearing a sheet, I told her I was kidnapped,
I asked her did she have a phone that I could
use because my purse was missing.

Her reply was "I don't have a phone, but I
will take you where you need to go?" At that
point I felt comfortable and knew I would be
going home. She told me to get in and she
will give me a ride home. At first I hesitated,
but I got in the car and told the woman
I lived two blocks down the road. I kept
starring at her because she seemed to have a
resemblance of someone I knew, I couldn't
remember who it was.

We approached my street going kind of fast,
I told her to turn right, she kept straight. I
looked out of the corner of my eye and her
facial expression had changed, she looked
very suspicious.

I kept saying, please stop here ma'am, right here, she kept driving. Suddenly she said "shut up before I kill you". I couldn't understand why the woman that seemed so nice was ignoring my plea; she kept driving at an increased rate of speed. I looked at the door lock with the thought of opening it and jumping out. The woman kept driving fast in a direction that contained woods, dirt, gravel and trees. I remained quiet for the safety of my life.

All of a sudden I said "miss what is your name"? Her reply was "shut up before I kill you"! The car stopped abruptly and the woman said "bitch you are lucky, I'm having a good day", she took her wig off and low and behold it was, the man that kidnapped me the night before. He said "I bet you won't ever steal again, now will ya"? My reply was "no"! I didn't want any disagreements with him; I just wanted to find a way out of that car. He stopped and said "get out". I asked him "where am I, I don't have any money to get home".

His reply was "not my problem", I begged
him to not leave me in the wooded area,
half clothed. He said "lady get out while
you have a chance, you're not my problem,
open the door". I was begging and pleading
with him to not leave me there, I opened the
door, stuck my leg out, he punched me in the
back of my head and shoved me out onto the
ground, then sped off.

As I sit on the side of the road crying and
asking God "why me, why is there so many
troubles in my way, I have been through
trials and tribulations with my family and
now troubles of my own. I did not know
what to do; I did not know what direction
to take, with no money. I began praying
humbly, thanking the lord for sparing my
life.

Now I know what mama meant when she
said we all go through storms in our lives
which could last a long time, but after it is
over then a brighter day will come, we must
keep the faith.

I began walking down this long narrow
rocky dirt road, singing "Jesus will work
it out, the problems that I have, I just can't
seen to solve them, I tried and I tried and my
problems seem to be getting worse, but when
I turned it over to Jesus, I stopped worrying
about it and he worked it out". I continued
walking and singing and before I knew it I
was at the end of the road.

I decided to sit and rest for a minute before I
continued my journey; I couldn't see where
I was going, because it was dark. I did not
know when I would make it home given the
fact that I was lost, but I felt the presence of
God walking right with me, I had no fear. I
walked all night, finally daylight came up
and I knew I would get help.

I looked up the road and I saw a building, I
couldn't tell if it was a home or business, but
I knew I was getting close. After walking ten
miles I finally made it, I knocked on the door
and it opened, the house was abandoned and
torn up inside with blown out windows.

I began to get discouraged but I knew I had to keep walking. After walking three miles, a truck with a lady and man came by; they stopped and asked me where I was going. My reply was "I'm trying to get home to my family, I was kidnapped two days ago and brought out here and shoved out of the car, and it's a long story". The lady said my name is "Maline and my brother's name is Mally, we're going fishing, can we take you somewhere? Do you need to go to the hospital? You seem to have been battered and bruised, how old are you"?

My reply was "Nineteen years old", I was afraid to accept the ride; I asked her if she had a phone, her reply was "I'm sorry I don't. I said in my mind, not another one, saying they don't have a phone. The lady saw how scared I was so she said "I see that you are afraid and shaking, we want to help you and we will make sure you get home, do you want to go to the hospital? Here let me show you my identification, I know you are traumatized right now and all we want to do is help you.

We are Christian people and we won't hurt you". After hearing the kind gesture from the people, I was still leery of accepting the ride but I needed to get home, suddenly I heard a voice in my head saying "I'm with you all the time, this is real, go home", I said "okay, I will accept the ride and I got in the truck.

I began praying hoping that the voice I heard was real and not another trap. I kept saying "God you are my strength, you told me you would never leave me". Maline, asked me "are you a Christian and do you go to church? My reply was "yes, I went to church when I was young, I haven't been in a while though, but I love the lord".

She told me she was looking for a church to attend. I told her about my old church, Heaven's Door Baptist Church. I told her once she enters, her life would immediately change. I also told her that I went there as a child but since I had been going through some hard times; I just haven't had time to go back.

Maline said "I thought the best time to go is when we are having hard times". I told her "true but, it's a long story, I can't explain it now".

Finally, I arrived home, it was a blessing to be back, I told the lord, even though I was a little scared, I knew he was always with me. I thanked Maline and Mally for being so kind and that I hoped to see them again. Mally said "ma'am you are a beautiful women, please do not allow yourself to be abused by anybody, stand up strong and say what you mean and mean what you say". My reply was "thanks for the ride".

After I relaxed, I called the rehab to talk to mama and LaLa, but I did not get an answer. I made continuous phone calls and still received no answer. I began wondering what the heck, was going on. I waited for several more hours then I called again, no answer. The next day I called no answer. I got very concerned because I knew I talked to them several weeks ago. No peace, No comfort!.

I couldn't remember where I left my car. I also had negative thoughts running through my mind, mama and LaLa could be dead, the rehab may have burned down, and I would never see them again. I had no good thoughts at this point.

I called the club and asked if a black 2005 Range Rover was in the parking lot and the reply was "yes", I said "oh my gosh, just knowing it was there for all those days took a load off my mind"! I asked my self, now what do I do, I knew I didn't have any money to ride the bus.

I had no choice but to call that unfaithful no good man, John. I asked him to come and take me to get my car; his reply was "where is your car"? I said "at the bar". He said "which bar" I told him "the Sharpen Iron Bar". He said "first of all, what were you doing at some sleaze bar and how did you leave your car there"? I told him "it is a long story, just come get me and take me to get my car". John told me he would come right away, but did not arrive until twelve midnight. Here we go again, he lied, I hate him, but I took the ride.

On the way to get my car, John told me
how much he missed me and how much
he loved me. He also said, before we go
get the car could we stop and talk. I knew
what his talking was all about. Part of me
wanted to say NO, but the other part wanted
something else. I kept thinking about him
being a married man and how wrong it was
to continue falling in the trap of his ungodly
acts.

I could not get my mind off him after he
took my virginity, I gave in and we stopped
behind a building and made out, in his car.
Afterwards he took me to my car; he thanked
me and told me to drive safely. I could not
believe a nice man like that were a liar and a
cheater.

As he began to leave, I asked him for ten
dollars for gas and he told me, "I don't give
woman my money" and he drove off. I felt
like a weak whore and a slut, how could I
have been so foolish? I continued to mess
with another woman's husband and he
treated me like trash. I felt violated, but I
knew I was wrong.

I'm out here in the dark, all alone and the car on empty. What do I do now? I began to think about mama saying we reap what we sow, I did not know what that meant, but now I see whatever I do, whether positive or negative it will come back on me. I started praying and asking God to forgive me one more time for my weakness and sin, I didn't think he would, but I would ask anyway. Lastly, I also asked him to get me home safely.

Morning came; I called the rehab, no answer. I drove to the place and the building was abandoned. I couldn't believe what I was seeing, the rehab building was abandoned, where is my mama and sister? I immediately began praying for peace in the mist of all the trials, tribulations and troubles I had been experiencing. I'm only nineteen and my life had been a living hell. What do I do now, my mama and sister were missing?

I called the police department, missing persons bureau and they told me the rehab relocated out of town, I was furious!

I asked the representative, how long had
the business been gone and why wasn't I
notified, because I had family in there. She
said "I don't know but take this number and
call for your self, goodbye". The person
didn't seem to care about, what I was talking
about. I immediately called and the voice
on the other end seemed very strange, I
identified myself and asked to speak to my
mother Janice Sorento or my sister Lala
Sorento. I was informed, no one was there
and the phone hung up.

I called again and the phone hung up, I
thought there was a bad connection so I
called again, no answer. Now, I'm really
wondering what's going on, where is my
mama and sister? I called the third time, and
the person on the other end said "lady, I told
you, no one by that name here".

I decided to ask for an address, the person
said "hold on" I waited ten minutes, a man
returned to say "may I help you"? I told him
I was trying to locate my mother and sister,
Janice and LaLa Sorento. He said "they are
not available" and hung up the phone.

Now I'm furious because everybody is telling me they are unavailable and I had no location for the rehab. I arrived back home with total frustration, I got the liquor from behind the bar and started sipping to calm my nerves, I drank the whole bottle. No Peace! No Comfort!

Morning came, I had a huge headache and no energy, I started crying loudly asking God "what happen to me, why am I having so many troubles, what did I do God to deserve this, help me lord, help me lord"! The voice in my head said "your faith is being tested, are you strong or weak, do you believe me"?

I kept hearing over and over in my head "I am the light, the alpha and the omega, the beginning and the end, you must keep on the whole armor and your sword in your hand to fight the demons that attack you everyday". I said God "what am I not doing"? "I have had trials, tribulations and troubles, all my life, this shouldn't be happening to me".

The voice said "your strength and faith is being tested to see if you are walking in the path of rightcousness, are you a strong warrior or are you weak"?

I stopped crying and began thinking, where could my mama and sister be. Day after day, I called the rehab; at least I thought that was where I was calling. Months passed, they still remain missing. I called the Federal Bureau of Investigations Office and filed a missing person's form, after two weeks, I received a call, asking me if I found my family.

My reply was "No and who was I talking to"? The voice said "ma'am, my name is Officer Stuplo, I have some disturbing news for you, but before I get into that, I need to ask you, what do you know about the place where your mother and sister is supposedly residing"? My reply was "a drug recovery rehab", he said "is that what they told you", and my reply was "yes" that's why I admitted my mama and sister, so they could recover from drugs".

Officer Stuplo went on to say "you must have been given the wrong information because that place is a home for atheist, they worship hatred. My investigations do not show any resident members by the name, Janice and LaLa Sorento. I started hollering and crying "where are they, where are they, what happened to them"? Officer Stuplo said "I can't help you" and hung up the phone. "Now what do I do" I asked myself? No peace! No Comfort!

Three more months passed, still no whereabouts of my mama and sister, I called Officer Stuplo and I was informed he did not work at the Office of Investigations anymore. I explained to the person the reason for my call, I informed her that Officer Stuplo told me that the drug rehab that my mother and sister was admitted to months ago appeared to be a Klu Klux Klan type establishment.

I also told her the rehab was suppose to be a drug recovery place by the name of Kutthroat Rehab Inc., located at 1231 Pushemup Blvd.

The representative's reply was "the only place listed at that address was Underground Railroad and they relocated to 37962 Waydown Railway Rd". I couldn't believe what I heard; I began to wonder if it was my fault for them missing, I was completely misled. I said to myself "now what do I do, Lord talk to me, I need to hear from you! I can't live like this, everyday . . . . trials, tribulations and troubles, I'm messed up, have been messed up, no where to turn, no one to love me, I'm all alone".

Suddenly the voice in my head said "so I guess I'm nobody, but let the truth be told, I'm everything. I created the earth, trees, people, animals and I know what to do and how to do, you have to have faith, belief and you must trust me. Always ask for what you want and it may be granted or may not. I am the ultimate decision maker, you must trust me my child, trust me".

At this point, I felt like I had lost everything . . . .

Mama and LaLa still missing, all of a sudden
I began feeling light headed with pains in my
stomach. I felt that because of all the stress
that I had been under, my blood pressure was
probably up from poor eating. After several
days, I decided to go to the doctor because
I did not feel any better; he requested that I
get blood drawn. I waited hours before I was
seen. Finally my name was called, the doctor
told me to wait because he was going to get
my results from my lab test.

I couldn't understand why it would take
so long to get lab results and why I would
even need a test for high blood pressure
and indigestion. I started thinking weird
thoughts, saying to my self "do I have
cancer, diabetes, HIV or heart trouble"?
The doctor stepped back in and I asked
him "what's the problem do I had cancer,
diabetes or heart trouble, which one. His
reply was "none of them, you're pregnant". I
told him that could not be true, I was on birth
control. His reply was "you are pregnant, the
test indicated you are and here's your card
for your next appointment".

As I left his office, I started crying, as if I didn't have enough problems already, now I'm pregnant. I don't know who the father is; could it be John's or the man that raped me? I couldn't wait to get home to get a drink to calm my nerves. I have to make decisions now, whether I will have the child or abort. I wanted to call my pastor but was too embarrassed to tell him, what I had been doing. I said to myself, I will do this all alone, I don't need his help. He is nobody; he can't help me, so forget him.

I put some potatoes on to boil, I continued to drink because it calmed my nerves, my spirit and it felt so good, one sip after another. I passed out and woke up three hours later to a house filled with smoke. I got scared, but glad to know it was only the pot burning. I began to think about how the neighbors across the street, didn't even come check to see if I was alright. I knew they were at home, but I also knew I cursed the family out the day before for parking their car on my side of the street; I didn't care though because I don't need them.

Well, a whole year passed since I heard from my mama and my sister. I'm four months pregnant and all alone. Nobody loves me, not even God. He said he did, but if he loved me he wouldn't have let all the horrible things happen to me, I'm beginning to wonder if he is real.

I thought about, if God was the man everybody says he is, then why do he sit and ignore me when I have a problem, he don't love me, I believe he is playing me. I have prayed over and over and he has not given me any attention. I continue to struggle everyday, and more when I pray.

I asked him to help me with all my problems and all he tells me is keep the faith. Faith is not what I need right now, I need to find my mama and sister they're whereabouts are still unknown, I didn't know whether to give up or continue looking. The voice in my head said "winners never quit and quitters never win, you are not a quitter. You need to get back to the principles of the bible for direction.

Where have all your faith gone he asked?
You use to be a young woman with plenty of
strength". I knew that was God talking to me
again, but I didn't want to hear that. I wanted
peace and quietness, so I took several drinks
to calm my nerves; I needed to take the load
off, I was under to much stress. I'm pregnant
don't know who the daddy is, mama and
sister missing, boyfriend lied to me and I
was raped by a man that said he had HIV, I
can't handle this life!

I kept drinking one shot after another. I
began to feel better. I didn't have any more
worries. I feel asleep and the next morning
I had a terrible headache, I couldn't get up,
my head was spinning and spinning; no
energy, sick in the stomach and throwing up.
I knew I had a hangover and I felt miserable.
I remembered hearing someone say, the
way to cure a hangover is to take another
drink, so that's what I did. I will take care
of myself; I don't need anybody telling me
about what God said.

I put the music on and it made me drink more. I ran out of Hennessey but found some Gin, I took some straight shots. I wasn't worried about being pregnant because, if God wanted me to have that baby he would take care of it and let me continue drinking; I was getting close to my delivery date anyway.

Well, the day came; I had a baby girl with facial features of an African American and Chinese. I was glad to get through that horrible pain. I noticed the baby whom I named Hennesy, after the liquor I drank the whole time I was pregnant, had shakes, terrible movements like seizures and excessive crying while she slept. The doctor told me after running test, that she was born alcohol addicted; he also asked me did I know anything about that. I told him, no.

I lied because I feared I would go to jail for ignoring the fact, I was pregnant and kept drinking. I didn't even want that child; I tried to get rid of it, hoping the liquor, would make me miscarriage.

Now I fear I will pay for what I've done. I still don't know who the father is. The doctor made the statement that, that child had liver and pancreas dysfunction. I began crying because I knew I was trapped, nobody want to baby-sit a handicapped kid. I need to live my own life; I asked the lord why did he do this to me? I know God created this problem. I am all alone and nobody to help me.

I called John and told him that I had that baby and he immediately said it wasn't his and hung up the phone. I called him again, he answered and said quit calling me and go fine your baby's daddy and hung up again. By this time, I was very mad, he took my virginity and now he doesn't want to talk to me, he used me, that baby continued to shake. I can't handle all this, so I took a drink, one after another.

I was so hurt to know John disowned that child. I took a paternity test to see who the father was and it was John's. I was enthused to know it was his, and not the man that raped me. No HIV! No worries!

After three months that child continues to
shake, my mother and sister still missing
and I have an extreme drinking problem. I
don't know what to do, I didn't want a child,
I don't have time for a child, and I'm too
young for this. I began to get very bored with
the hassle of taking care of a crying child, no
help just me all alone.

I heard this voice once again in my head
saying "what happen to you, you have totally
disobeyed what you have been taught, and
you are straddling the fence. You are still my
child and I haven't thrown you away, so why
are you lowering your dignity and neglecting
your duties as a mother"?

My reply was "I don't have time right now
to be held down, I never said I wanted a
child and anyway you're in my head so quit
talking to me". The voice replied "you need
to get back in church, and stop listening to
the enemy; you can not have two masters,
if you come back with me you will live,
prosper, grow and go to heaven.

If you stay on the path that you're going you
will fall so low you will not be able to get up
so easily, you have to come back to me, if
you want to live". I told him "it's too hard to
follow you, God"! The reply was "when you
are ready to have faith, peace, happiness, joy
and strength in your life, get on your knees
and ask for forgiveness for your sins, that's
all I ask you to do, BUT you must be ready
for change when you come to me.

You can't see it now, but that day will come.
I will always be there for you". I didn't want
to hear all that, what else could possibly
happen to me?

Well, another year passed more trials,
tribulations and troubles, no peace, no
comfort, no end!

I received more disturbing news, this time
by mail. I couldn't understand why a letter
would be sent with no name, just the words
H.E.L.P and no return address. I began to
wonder if it could be mama or LaLa trying to
get in touch with me. "Something is wrong",
I said. "Where do I start"?

I wanted to call on Jesus but I didn't feel he was the answer because I called him before and he ain't done anything yet. That man let me down; I really didn't believe there was a God anymore.

When I was young all I heard mama say, trust and believe, well I did that and look what happened, all lies. Here I am stuck with a child that is a year old and can't even walk or talk. I have had many struggles every since I turned sixteen. I'm tired of this life! All I do is drink and cry, what a way to live. I am tired of that child hollering, all the time.

Another month passed and another letter came with the same words . . . H.E.L.P! I called the Federal Bureau Investigations and told them about the letter, I also asked if I could have that rehab investigated because my mama and sister had been missing too long. The voice on the other end said I would have to make an appointment and speak to a representative about my concerns.

I filed the paperwork and it took six weeks
to receive a response. The letter stated an
investigation would start within the week.
I felt better because I knew I would get an
answer soon after the investigation was
complete. I hoped that the day mama and
Lala are found they would be alive and well.
It's been years since I seen them.

Where is my peace I asked, as I took a drink,
all Hennesscy do is cry. I can't pick her up,
so I will close the door and let her cry herself
to sleep, I don't have time for a child. I
began thinking about how I could get rid of
her and not get in trouble. Then I thought of
leaving her on someone's doorstep or even at
the fire station.

Suddenly that darn voice in my head said
"did I leave you"? I told the voice "you go
away, that's why I'm in the shape I'm in
right now"! The voice continued to say "my
child you have fallen by the way side and
your faith have faltered, but you can change.
I ask you not harm your child anymore; quit
drinking and most of all seek some spiritual
advice for your problems".

"Being able to bear a child is a gift from me,
I made you and I allowed you to make her,
but you did not follow my word properly and
now you must suffer the consequence".

The Ten Commandments said, "Thou shall
not commit adultery. You did not listen
and you did not care, knowing that alcohol
would endanger the fetus, you kept drinking,
excessively. You we're selfish, disobedient
and weak. You must stop allowing the enemy
to control you, or you will not prosper.
You can not have two masters, positive and
negative; you have to make a choice".

"Come back to me and I will renew your
strength". I kept thinking about what I
heard in my head, I can't serve two masters,
positive and negative. I didn't know I was
serving two masters, I didn't consider the
devil as my master and the way God was
treating me, he didn't act like he wanted to
be my master either. My life has too many
trials, tribulations and troubles, so maybe I'll
try and change.

I decided I would go to church on Sunday,
but on Saturday night I went out to the club,
me and that child. I sat her in the corner in
her car seat while I boozed and danced the
night away. When the time came to go home,
I was stoned. I got in my car and drove off,
I did not make it into the house, I passed out
in the drive way.

Morning came, the sun shining bright and
I was still in the car. I went into the house
and took another drink. All of a sudden, I
heard a very loud knock at the door, it was
the police. The officer identified himself as
Detective Beatumdown, he asked me if I had
a baby girl by the name of Hennessey.

I told him yes and asked him why was he
there. He said "the owner of the Midnight
Bar called to report a baby left under a table
and footprints show you are the mother".
I said "what, I didn't leave no child at no
club". The officer stated "where is your
baby"? My reply was "In her room sleep".
He said "may I see her" I ran to her room
and it was empty. I began crying because I
knew I was going to jail.

The police said "you are under arrest for child abandonment; you will be able to explain to the judge why your child was left there. I begged and pleaded for the officer to not take me, I also told him I would go down the next morning and give a statement. He told me that he had to take me. I tried to make obscene gestures to him in hopes of him letting me go. That didn't work . . . .

I arrived at the police department and I saw many people that looked like me. I couldn't understand how I could go from being an honor student to a lowdown wretch. As I sat waiting for my name to be called I thought about how stupid I had been. I done had many trials, tribulations and troubles, gave my womanhood up before marriage, I have a fatherless child with birth defects, I am an alcohol abuser and I'm selfish, it's my fault.

I was a model citizen, but look at me now. All I do is drink myself to sleep every night and continue to pour liquor in an innocence baby's bottle. She ain't even walking, two years old, can't talk and still in diapers. I don't have time for this; I'm too young to be raising a child.

I heard that voice say again "when we make mistakes knowingly, consequences will come; you will have to pay for that. I ask that you repent and learn from this. You said you didn't want a child, you must be careful what you ask for, now she is out of your life", but you are not free, either".

When the judge called my name, she had a facial expression of a pit bull. She asked me why I took my child to a club, I told her I was not going to be there long and I just wanted to get away for a while, I also told her I did not have a babysitter.

Wrong answer . . . .

The judge told me that was no excuse and I was an unfit mother, she also said I would never see my child again. She said she would make sure I stay locked up many years for hurting her. While she was talking, I was praying, I asked God to help me, I know I had not been obedient and if he helps me out of this trouble, I would never do it again. I told the judge that I didn't mean to leave her there; I had a little too much to drink and didn't remember.

No sympathy . . . .

I continued to tell the judge, I've had so
many problems in the last few years, I
just forgot. She said "SHUT UP, you will
remain in jail until you rot, your fine is fifty
thousand dollars and you will attend a twelve
step program and many more, get her out of
my court room"!

I couldn't believe what I was hearing, all
that just for one little thing. The voice in
my head said "my child, that is no excuse,
you shouldn't have had a child if you didn't
want the responsibility of being a parent.
I still love you because I gave you life,
but you have to know and learn from this
experience".

I was escorted to my cell and as soon as I got
there I was told I would get beat up because
I was a child abuser. I didn't understand how
she knew that. I decided to lie down on my
cot, I fell asleep and started dreaming about
me being in prison for the horrible things I
did to my child.

I was sentenced eighteen years, one year for every year of Hennessey's life until she was an adult. Since I made an innocent child suffer through birth and a year after, the judge added two more years. Twenty years locked up with no chance of parole, all I could do was cry, because I knew my life was over.

Suddenly, I heard my name being called; I jumped up and was relieved to know I was only dreaming. The warden told me to get up and go to my program. As I was being escorted, the other jailers were trying to grab me through the bars of the cell, I was very frightened. When I got to the program, I was told to sit down, lay my hands on my lap and keep my mouth shut.

I didn't have to be told that because I did not want to open my mouth anyway. The officer in charge of the group called my name and told me that I had to attend several programs before I would be eligible for bail. I could not imagine what kind of programs that would be, I didn't kill anybody.

The program consisted of twelve weeks of
anti-alcohol learning classes; faith-based
learning sessions and I had to go work at
a morgue for abused deceased children for
two months. I was completely terrified, I
began crying and asking God why was he
punishing me so hard? I didn't deserve that, I
didn't kill that child, I just made a mistake.

The voice in my head stated "you must
understand I love you, but you can't
have two masters. Look at you now, you
disobeyed my word and it landed you in
a world of destruction. You still have the
chance to change, start now. You must begin
with the truth; you have a daughter that you
do not acknowledge, that is against me".

"You have lost your faith, belief and strength
and that too is against me. Open up your
bible and start reading the word again, it will
lead you in a positive direction, it will renew
and reconnect your mind with wisdom, and
you will have a new beginning in life. You
must be obedient unto the word, and stop
trying to handle everything yourself, I am
the Alpha and the Omega, the beginning and
the end".

I decided to pay attention to the voice, I
asked the guard for a bible and his reply
was "are you really going to read it"? I said
"yes, I've had so many trials, tribulations
and troubles in my young life and since
I stopped reading the word and going to
church, nothing have worked. I remember
when mama use to take me and my sister
every Sunday, I followed rules, my heart was
humbled, I cared about others, I had faith
and belief, and I did real well, but look at me
now".

He told me "you will never lose it; you just
need to renew it". I felt very good when he
told me that because the voice in my head
said the same thing, if I renew my faith I will
renew my strength, then I will renew my
belief and I will renew my life.

Even though I couldn't understand what the
bible was saying, I turned to Romans 8:1-2,
Colossians 1:27 and 1 Corinthians 6:19
which read, "I speak to you from the depths
of your being. Hear me saying soothing
words of peace, assuring you of my love.

"Do not listen to voices of accusations,
for they are not from me. I speak to you
in love-tones, lifting you up. My spirit
convicts cleanly, without crushing words
of shame. Let the spirit take charge of your
mind, combing out tangles of deception. Be
transformed by the truth that I live within
you. The light of my presence is shining
upon you, in benedictions of peace".

"Let my light shine in you; don't dim it
with worries or fears. Holiness is letting me
live through you. Since I dwell in you, you
are fully equipped to be holy. Pause before
responding to people or situations, giving my
spirit space to act through you. Hasty words
and actions leave no room for me".

"I want to inhabit all your moments-gracing
your thoughts, words, and behavior". I took
verse by verse, wrote it down and re-wrote
it in my words, it gave me a complete
understanding. Day after day I went to my
programs, just as I entered into the morgue
for deceased children fear took over my soul.

The person in charge took me and showed
me all the children that had died from
parent abuse and neglect. I got teary eyed
because I did not realize so many children
were abused. I saw babies with burn marks,
missing limbs, gun shot wounds, rope burns,
holes in different parts of their body and
even holes in their eyes; I got sick looking at
that.

I told the man, "I can't stay here" he said
"you have no choice, remember you made
the decision, to neglect your child. You
thought the wild life was the way to go, but
look where it got you. I will also tell you
that if you don't change your actions, you
will suffer even more. You are sitting here
thinking only about you and your child is in
foster care, two years old functioning on a
three month old level".

"I don't want to seem harsh, but you were
sent here to work and that is what you will
do, Let this be a lesson learned. You have
two months to complete before you are
eligible to go home, so put your gloves on
and get started to work".

Chapter Three

"TROUBLES"

Well, one month passed and I still have one to go. My life is very shallow, no peace, no comfort, no freedom . . . .

As I read the words from the bible over and over, I began to gain a clear understanding of what was being said. I sit in my cell, day after day with nothing to do but read and pray. In the beginning, I thought it was not necessary, but now I see everything else I was doing didn't work either. Now I'm forced to read and pay attention to the word.

I turned to Matthew 6:24; Revelation 2: 4; Ephesians 3:16-17; and Psalms 16: 11 and it said "You cannot serve two masters, If I am truly your Master; your desire is to please me above all others. If pleasing people or self becomes a priority to you, you will be forever enslaved by them or it".

"Living creatures and substances can be harsh taskmasters, when you give them power over you. If I am the Master of your life, I will be your first love. You serving me allow you to be rooted, grounded and unconditional".

"The lower you bow down before me, the higher I lift you up into intimate relationship with me. The joy of living in my presence outshines all other pleasures. I want you to reflect my joyous light by living in increasing intimacy with me".

I went to the morgue and I saw a child that was badly decomposed due to his parent killing him and stuffing his body under the porch of the house. All I could do was cry and ask the lord for forgiveness for all the sins that I created, I asked him to please give me another chance to get it right. I really didn't feel God was listening to me because I created so many sins, not only for me but my helpless child.

Now because of me, Hennessey may not have a normal life. I attended my bible group class and I testified that I wanted to change my life. I wanted to show the world that I could be a good parent. I also told them, I saw the abused deceased children that did not even have a chance to live, I must change and I will.

Finally, two months passed and I got released, until my court date was set. I made it home and now I am back in the same atmosphere that I left. I saw the liquor on the bar, I thought about taking a drink but something in my head said "do you really want to go backwards, you said you wanted to move in a positive direction, here is your chance". I took the bottles and poured them out because I felt the voice in my head, was God watching everything I do.

Instead of cooking I decided to go eat at the neighborhood restaurant, I saw a flyer on the table and heard people talking about a church by the name of Powerhouse Baptist, that was on and popping with a dynamic pastor. I continued to listen and then I told them I was looking for a church home, they were so eager to give me the name and location.

Sunday morning came; I was inspired to get ready for the service. I approached the door and the presence of the members was so warm; they greeted me and escorted me to my seat.

I felt I had another chance to repent and start a new life. After church was over, I knew it was no accident, for me to be in the right place, at the right time to find my new church home.

Two weeks passed, I decided to continue in my therapy as well as volunteering at the children's home on a regular basis. I wanted to get all the training I could, I also wanted to show the courts that I was trying to gain knowledge for proper parenting.

After six months, I now have a pillar of faith and strength, under the biblical leadership of Pastor Lightenbug. Now, I can hold my head up high, and walk in faith; I regained my belief, strength, and joy. I know I must follow the words in the bible, stay in church and serve in the community. I also know obstacles will continue to come my way but, I will know how to handle them.

I started shouting "hallelujah, hallelujah, thank you Jesus, I'm a person again. I strayed away but I came back, it's all because of you God"!

"I know my mama taking me to church when I was young was the beginning. Lord I didn't forget, I knew I was a good person. Now I have to make everything right with you. I have to get my child back and become the mother she never had. I will cherish and love her even if she doesn't ever have a normal life, I will sacrifice my life for her".

I went home to a lonely house, I felt like a queen. The telephone rang and it was John. Part of me wanted to show anger for what the hurtful things he done to me, but I knew with my new life and trusting in God, I needed to maintain my dignity. I said "how are you" his reply was "I'm alright, it could be better" I went on to ask him "what's wrong and how's your family"?

I remained calm because I know I didn't have power to change anything, only God did. I felt, talking to John might just lead him to Christ. His reply was "I don't have a family anymore, the wife left me. I needed somebody to talk too, so I decided it was you". He also asked me "how my child was was doing?

I told him, she was in a temporary foster home; I abused her due to my selfish ways. I also told him, that I went to jail because I left her in the club. He was not surprised to hear everything I told him. He said "I know most of what you went through was because of me, I told you numerous lies, I disowned my child and now I'm paying for all of it, I lost everything, I live in a room behind my job". I began to feel sorry for him, but I could not help him, only God could.

I told him that I changed my life and I worship at a wonderful church and if he would like to go, his life would change too. I gave him the name, location and time and told him to try God and he will prosper. He looked at me funny and said "me going to church, I have never been to church". I told him "well, it's time to go". John asked me if he could come over and talk to me, my flesh wanted to say yes, but I knew it was not the right thing to do, so I told him "NO".

He said "you have changed, because you have never turned me down". My reply was "I have strength now, I can stand up and say what I mean and mean what I say".

"I will not allow the devil to destroy what God and I have going on. He treats me better than any man I know, he's my daddy and my daddy loves me for real, my daddy doesn't take advantage of me. He provides me instruction for success; I have to read the bible everyday. I didn't understand it at first, but going to bible study corrected my misunderstanding. He tells me the proper way of life and if I don't listen to him, consequences will follow". John, seek God and watch your life move in a positive direction. See ya Sunday".

A letter came in the mail from the child protective service, informing me of my court date. At first, I had fear but the new person in me; knew fear was not part of my new beginning. I repented to God and that was confirmation enough for me to handle what ever came my way. I prayed and asked the lord for forgiveness and I knew he forgave me.

I walked into the court room with my head held high and knew God, my daddy was with me.

I began hearing these words in my head "fear not, today is the day that the I hath made, rejoice and be glad in it". I kept hearing it over and over. Now that I know that voice is God, I asked him "what are you telling me"? His reply was "I made this day, you can relax, be happy because I got this covered.

The other judge that told me, she would lock me up for twenty years, was out on extended sick leave. My lawyer informed me that she was biased and I wouldn't have gotten a fair trial. He said "you see I helped you out", I told him "thank you, but God already had told me to relax because he was in charge".

An appointee by the name of Judge Sa-vi-or read my case and asked me how did I feel? My reply was "I'm blessed, I'm blessed, I'm blessed, that's all I can say, I'm blessed". He also asked me had I learned from my mistakes. My reply was "yes, my daddy in heaven had already given me a new beginning in life, but I didn't accept my wrong doings until I went to jail. Now all I want to do is get my child back and be the mother, I've never been.

After a brief period of silence, the judge
said "this is the first time you've had
any problems with the law, you will pay
restitution in the amount of five-hundred
dollars, fifty hours community service, fifty
hours alcohol abuse education class and you
will take a parenting course". He continued
by saying "I truly believe you are sincere
and won't repeat this behavior. If you come
back again, you will not have the benefit that
you have today. Once you complete all your
programs, your case will be closed; you will
get your child back. You must return back
to my office within four months, with the
proof, this court is adjourned".

I gained more strength than ever when I
walked out of the courtroom. I told God,
"you are so awesome, you told me you had
my back and you did. I love you daddy".
Now I have peace and comfort, I know how
to handle trials, tribulations and troubles.

I signed up for everything, at once. I wanted
to learn all I could, especially learning how
to be a responsible and loving parent.

I prayed that I didn't damage my child's life,
but if I did I would take care of her and love
her, for the rest of my life. I called the foster
care home and they told me she was doing
well, but I would not be able to see her until
I was released by the judge. Just knowing
I would be able to see her again, gave me
strength to finish all my duties. Suddenly, I
began to smile.

Sunday morning came; I was still tired after
working my community service. I didn't feel
like getting up for church. I thought about
how nice it would be to sleep in for once. I
continued to lay there with my eyes closed.
Suddenly the voice in my head said "you
must get up and go to the house of the Lord,
you must be obedient".

I continued to lie down and all of a sudden
I jumped up, I remembered that I told John
I would be there. I did not want to minister
to him and not abide by the word myself. I
made it to the church and could not believe
my eyes, when I saw him standing in front
of the church, I said to my self, God Thank
you! John and I began praising and listening
to the word from the pastor.

After church, John told me he enjoyed himself so much and it was a new experience, he also said he would come again. All of a sudden he asked me when he could see our child. I told him after I finished my community service and paying all the money owed; I would be granted my baby back.

He asked me "how much do you owe" my reply was "five-hundred dollars". John got quiet and then said "I have to make my life right, so I will start by paying the money for you". I could not believe what I was hearing, but I said "thank you". I began to wonder if he wanted something in return. I asked him "John why are you helping me pay the money? If you want something from me, it is not going to happen".

He said "I asked God to forgive me for my sins and I felt a good way to start, would be to help you, you are in need right now and I do have a child with you". He continued saying "I don't want anything from you; I just want to make things right with all the people I have caused heavy burdens upon".

"I know I have a long ways to go, but I will change my life. I know you might not believe this, but I developed feelings for you, but it was wrong how I did it. I know you must hate me, but I ask you to please let me be in my child's life". I told him "once you make it right with God, everything else will fall in place and you will be in your child's life, this life is new for both of us".

I said to John "I want to spend every minute, every hour and every day caring for our child, I neglected her when she was born and I'm not proud of that. I don't know if she will have the opportunity to live a normal life, but what I do know is that God have forgiven me for my sins". Tears came to my eyes, as I continued to think about how my disobedience and unearthly selfish character caused me to abuse and neglect my child.

I know one day I will have to explain why she ended up in foster care. I said to myself, Lord, will I be ready for that? I don't know if I will be able to explain to her, how her life began.

The Lord replied "when the time comes, you will know exactly what to say, for now stay focused and watch me work". I began to smile because I knew the trials, tribulations and troubles that I had been through, happened for a reason. Even though I wouldn't be able to see her until I finished my community service, I knew my new life as a parent would start soon. I am so grateful because my mind, body and soul had been cleansed.

Two months passed, I returned back to Judge Sa-vi-or and he informed me that I completed my task within the timeframe; he also said I was very skilled and obedient and because of that he would order for my baby to return home soon, with a full time provider for thirty days, she would monitor and make sure I was following parenting procedures.

I had a daring look on my face, because he said she would return soon, he didn't give me an exact date. He also said I had to be monitored; I didn't need anybody standing over me and telling me what to do. I thought I would be free to be a parent.

I heard the voice say "you must have patience this is a test, are you going to pass or fail"? I kept quiet because I didn't want to blow my chance of getting my child back. The Judge informed me that I would have additional parenting classes which would include anger management and child discipline. He said after I complete that thirty day program, I would be ready to take Hennessey home.

I asked the judge if her father could go with me, his reply was "yes he may". I immediately said "thank you very much". The judge asked me if I had any more questions, my reply was "no sir", he said "this court is adjourned". I couldn't wait to call John and tell him what the judge said.

I asked him if he would like to go to classes with me, his reply was "sure I will go, I need to learn how to be a loving parent too, I never showed any love to my other children. I played mind games with my ex-wife and I told one lie after the other, now she hates me.

Chapter Four

"TRIUMPH"

John continued by saying "I hope one day I will have the opportunity to apologize to her, with sincere words and with hopes of her accepting it". I feel very bad because I think about all the people I manipulated, used and abused. I immediately started feeling different about John because he wanted to do what was right, not only for Hennessey, but his other children.

I thanked the Lord, because I really didn't feel like John would even accept my invitation to come to church, now I realized that with God all things are possible. What a Blessing!

The time has finally come . . . .

I went to court with peace and joy, knowing the outcome would be positive. I changed my life, I ministered and brought my friend to Christ, I completed all my restitution, community service and is clean from alcohol, so I have no fear. I knew I was blessed because I now had power over my life. I renewed my faith and I had not doubts about my child being returned.

I waited calmly for the judge to enter, I had
smiles all over my face. All of a sudden
the bailiff told us to stand and in walked
that Judge Grossum, my heart immediately
started beating fast because I remembered
her telling me I would never see daylight
or freedom again. The voice in my head
said "Isaiah 8:13 says Do not fear anything
except the Lord Almighty". I lifted my head
and said "thank you Lord, I leave it in your
hands".

When my name was called I stepped up,
greeted the judge, with no doubt. She asked
me did I finish paying my restitutions and
community service. My reply was "yes".
She said "I see that you have satisfied the
court in its entirety, so your case is closed".
She also stated the case worker would return
my child in two hours. I began shouting
and crying with joy because I listened to
what the voice in my head told me, that is
confirmation, how powerful God is. I rushed
home to get Hennessey's room ready, when
the phone ranged, it was John asking if he
could come see me. I told him yes, because I
knew he was a changed man.

I told John that I was glad he called and it was perfect timing because our baby girl was coming home. I heard the joy in his voice as he said "I'll be right over". I sat with hesitation; I decided to open the bible to Psalm 107: 1-2, I read "give thanks to the Lord, for he is good! His faithful love endures forever. Has the Lord redeemed you? Then speak out! Tell others he has saved you from your enemies".

I thought that was a powerful statement, I also thanked the Lord for teaching me how to live again, for renewing my soul, showing me a different way, showing me how to love, trust and serve him with all my heart. I can say I went through a season of discomfort, trials, tribulations and troubles but now I know it's my season.

Ding dong the door bell ranged, it was the caseworker, Hennessey and John . . . . What a reunion! I felt like God gave me another chance at being a mother. Hennessey was three years old; she held her hands out for me, as if she already knew who I was.

I immediately took her in my arms with a tight embrace and saying "I'm your mommy, I missed you so much and I love you". I also pointed at John and said "daddy, this is yo daddy". John and I began playing, when all of a sudden Hennessey said "ma-me and da-d, my mama and daddy".

Tears kept streaming from our eyes because she accepted us as her parents. I paid close attention to my baby and I saw that she had overcome all her birth defects She could walk, talk and was potty trained.

The caseworker said "well I will leave you wonderful family to bond; I'm not needed here anymore". I said "what, you're not staying for four weeks"? She said "no, I was told to observe how the child adapted to the environment and make a determination if I needed to stay.

I don't see a reason to remain in the home; Hennessey is very blessed to have two loving parents. I will revisit in three months, don't hesitate to call me if you need to, otherwise take care of her and love her like we did, have a wonderful day"

Three months passed and I can't believe my
life is so pleasant, no stress, no anger, no
disobedience. I can't believe I have a life,
I'm a mother of a child that I love so much,
I also know that life has its ups and downs,
but now that I am walking in the path of
righteousness, God have given me so much
faith and strength.

Now that I am settled in, I'm trying to be a
perfect role model for Hennessey, but I am
terrified because I know if I make a mistake
I might go back to jail and lose her again.
I know I don't have all the answers and
I'm not strong mentally, but I have a strong
person on my side that gives me faith, GOD!

I began praying "father I ask you today to
stand with me and give me a lot of strength,
patience and understanding so I can raise my
child, also God thank you for her not having
any birth defects, Amen"!

Just as I finished my prayer the phone
ranged, it was John asking me how his two
ladies were doing. I said to my self, his two
ladies.

What is he talking about, I guess he know
something I don't. My reply to him was
"Hennessey and I are doing great, how have
you been doing, long time, no hear from".
He said "working and going through, but
thru it all I still have joy from the lord,
I found him and I will continue to trust
him through all my trials, tribulations and
troubles".

He continued to say "I have to stand up
and accept all my faults. I know this is a
test of my faith and to see if I will abide by
the word. I also know that I have to face
consequences from the life that I use to live".
I asked him, "John why hadn't I heard from
you before now and why haven't you been
to church"? His reply was "I had to get the
courage to call you; I didn't want you to
think of me like I was in the past".

"I have been dealing with my baby's mama,
whom does not believe in the lord, so you
know that was drama. I stand strong because
I created the problem and I have learned
that I reap what I sow. I lost family and
friends because of my new life, but I gained
strength, I'm a new man saved by grace".

John continued to say, "now that I have a better understanding, I have accepted God as my family and friend, I have not been to church because of my working schedule, but I prayed and asked God to change it so I can actively participate". He also said "will you allow me to be your friend and a father to Hennessey"?

I was surprised but I immediately said "yes, please continue to move forward in what you want God to do for you in your life take care of all your children and you will reach tremendous heights". He said "may I see her"? My reply was "sure, she's in her play pen". The joy of seeing John embracing his daughter made me so happy. I know we are going to make great parents.

At seven o'clock pm, John approached me and asked if he could make a suggestion, my reply was "yes anytime". He said "now that we are new born Christians, why don't we change Hennessey's name, we don't want memories of our past to follow us in our new life. She is still very young so changing it now would be best".

I told him "that's a great idea, I was thinking
about the same thing, so what should
we name her"? He said "Miracle, she is
our miracle". I said "wow, John that is a
beautiful name and it fit her, you're right she
is a miracle, our miracle".

After a moment of silence I noticed John
starring at me with a lustful look on his face.
I began thinking in my mind, that's the same
look he had in the beginning and I wondered
if he would go back to his old ways even
though he said he had changed. I asked him
was something on his mind.

His reply was "yes, a matter of fact, I do
have something to say". I wondered what it
could be because; he said he wanted to be
a father to his child. I said "I'm listening"!
His reply was "thank you for leading me to
Christ". My reply was "you are so welcome,
but I have to give all the glory to God
because he led both of us to Christ. We came
together. We can continue to learn and praise
him together if you choose to go. A family
that prays together will remain together.

All of a sudden John said "you are my best friend, right? My reply was "right"; he then said "you enjoy my friendship, right? I said "yep". He said "that's not good enough for me; I want you to be my wife. We can continue growing together, serving God taking step by step until we are ready to go all the way and we will take our children to church with us. If you allow me to show you that I'm a changed man, we will be together forever".

I'm going to tell my ex-wife whom is a non believer of God that we will pick up the children and take them to church with us, they will be raised in a Christian environment, and Hennessey will know her siblings". I was shocked and glad at the sometime, John also said "we have a lot to work through and to work for, but I know with faith, we can do it".

"I have chosen you and if you choose me, we can move forward". We began embracing with tears and laughter, I told him "yes, I choose you", I'm so happy my life is moving in a direction of peace and happiness.

Three months have passed, John have taken
full responsibilities for our child, he started
paying child support and we started spending
more time together as a family. He asked
me if he could move in to save money. My
reply was "yes, I love you and I don't want
to spend another day away from you". I
couldn't believe what was happening to me,
all my trials, tribulations and troubles seem
to be turning around, at least I thought!

Later that evening after John left for work,
the phone rang it was a weird sounding voice
saying "I see you". I said "who is this", the
phone hung up. That was a very startling
feeling because I couldn't understand who
could be watching me.

I called John and left a message for him to
call me right away. I started hearing sounds
like someone was outside my house. I began
praying because I knew that the power of
prayer would protect me and my baby. I
began wondering if John's ex-wife could be
stalking me.

Several hours later the phone rung and it
was John asking me if I was o.k. I told him
that I was after I prayed, because I knew
God had a shield around baby and me. John
apologized for the delay, but he was driving
the forklift and didn't feel the vibration of
his phone. I told him I understood, because I
knew I had to stand on the word, myself for
protection.

John asked me if I wanted him to take off
from work to be with me. I told him that was
not necessary, I'm not afraid anymore, have
a great night. He told me he would come
over as soon as he got off work, we hung up.
I drifted off to sleep and began dreaming, I
saw the shadow of a person lurking outside
my windows, dressed in black clothing,
sunshades and a black sweater with a hoodie.

I thought the person resembled John's
ex-wife, but I couldn't tell. I stooped down
below the window ceil and continued, to see
what was happening. I thought the person
was trying to get in the window, but went to
the back door and began fondling the screen.

I called the police in a whisper voice and
told them I had intruders, I gave my address
and in minutes they were jumping the fence
into my back yard.

The officers caught the intruder, handcuffed
him or her and rung my door bell and
said ma'am do you know this man; he
was trying to get in your house. I took the
hoodie off his/her head and low and behold
it was John's ex-wife. She began crying
and hollering, saying I stole her man and
she hated me for it. I remained silent as the
officers carried her to the car, struggling.

When the sun came up, I woke up; I looked
around and was so relieved to know I was
only dreaming. I didn't mention it to John
because I wanted it to be over. I hoped that
the phone call that I received was a wrong
number, I've had enough!

John moved in and decided that instead of
waiting, we would marry and live right. We
tied the knot two weeks later and changed
our baby's name, on that day. I told John,
he and Miracle was the best thing that ever
happened to me.

I continue to tell john "we found God together, have a child together and now we're married and God is highly pleased. Our precious Miracle Jewel will be raised by two loving parents in a positive environment. I know obstacles will continue to come our way, but now we know how to trust that God will take care of it.

For the first time, I informed John that the house that we lived in belongs to my mother; she and my sister had been missing for several years. I continued to pray they would return home. John looked at me with a strange look because I never talked about that before. I felt it was time that he knew what was going on.

Three months passed, John, Miracle and I were eating dinner when all of a sudden the doorbell rang. I said "wonder who that could be?" I opened the door and it was mama and LaLa, I started screaming and crying, John came running with Miracle in his arms. He saw two ladies standing in the door; we were all starring at each other.

All of a sudden I said "mama and LaLa is
that you"? Both of them replied "yes", I
began hollering and saying, I missed you'll
so much. Come on in here and sit down,
we have so much to talk about". Mama and
LaLa looked so different; they both put
on some weight and showed no signs of
physical abuse.

I noticed mama looking at John and Miracle
with a strange look, she said "hello sir, how
are you, is that your child, she is beautiful"?
Johns reply was "I'm doing well ma'am, yes,
our precious Miracle is your granddaughter,
and I am her father".

Mama looked with a blank stare on her face,
all of a sudden she said "you had a baby,
you mean I'm a grandmother"? I said "yes
mama, you are a grandmother, her name is
Miracle Jewel and this is her father John,
my husband". Mama said "wow, a lot have
happened since I been gone, we sure do have
a lot to talk about. I am so happy to be home,
now I can start my life over, with God".

"I'm tired for now, LaLa and I broke out of that horrible place and walked all the way until we made it home. I couldn't remember the phone number and we didn't have any money to make a call anyway".

"The place where we were worshipped the devil, they tried to brainwash our minds and turn us into slaves for men. They controlled us, if we didn't do what they wanted us to do, they would beat us. I could not take that anymore. I told LaLa, we were women that were created by God and not to be used or abused".

"When the opportunity came, we left. We are so glad to be home; tomorrow we will catch up on what's been going on while I was away. I am a new person and I will never allow nothing and no one to destroy me again".

I told mama that John lived here but now that she and LaLa is back, we would find another home, but since she didn't have any income, John and I would stay until she get a job.

I also told her that the first thing we would do as a family is go to church, we had a lot be thankful for. John and I were new Christians practicing the word and reading the bible together. I began thinking about how blessed and how happy I was to be a child of the King. Mama, LaLa and I had been through so much, I didn't know if I would ever see them again, but God already showed me if I do his will, he will do mine.

I told mama that I prayed over and over for her and LaLa to be found alive. I believe that every since I went to church and decided to live right that is why many blessings have been coming my way. We are all together again, we've been through trials, tribulations, troubles and now God have given us triumph. **VICTORY IS MINE!**

**VICTORY IS MINE
VICTORY IS MINE
VICTORY TODAY IS MINE,
I TOLD SATAN GET THEE BEHIND
VICTORY TODAY IS MINE!**

"GOD WILL MULTIPLY OUR BLESSINGSWE HAVE A CHOICE"**

Jesus is the reason for the season; he will be with you and will never fail or forsake you. Do not fear or be dismayed.

Sincerely,

Vivian Lady "V" Lewis